LEARN ALONG WITH ARTHUR

Grade 1 Reading: Arthur at School

Table of Contents

Sequencing	2
Following Directions	3
Reading for Information/Deductive Reasoning	4
Sequencing	5
Reading for Information/Deductive Reasoning	6
Word Recognition: Beginning Sounds	7
Sight Words/Reading Words in Context	8
Word Identification	9
Following Directions	10, 11
Reading for Information/Deductive Reasoning	12, 13
Letter/Sound Correspondence	14
Sight Words/Rhyming	15
Compound Words	16, 17
Letter/Sound Correspondence	18
Matching Characters/Titles	19
ABC Order	20
Categorizing	21
Sight Words/Numbers	22
Opposites	23
Classification Skills	24, 25
Deductive Reasoning	26
Contractions	27
Conclusion	28
Glossary of Skills	29, 30
Answer Key	31, 32

TM and © 1999 Marc Brown. All Rights Reserved.

Sequencing

Arthur was excited about going to school. Last night he . . .

laid out his clothes   sharpened his pencils   packed his book bag

"I can't wait for tomorrow," Arthur said.
"I wonder what you'll forget to take," said D.W.

Put the pictures in order to show what Arthur did in the morning.

Arthur ate breakfast.   He waited for the bus.   Arthur got dressed.   Arthur woke up.

Following Directions

Arthur was proud of his new book bag. It was red. It had yellow and blue shapes.
"This is a great book bag for school," Arthur said at breakfast.
"It better have a rocket booster," said D.W. "You're late."

Follow the directions below to see what Arthur's new book bag looks like.

Draw a zipper on Arthur's book bag. Color the straps black.
Decorate Arthur's backpack with yellow  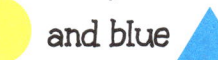 and blue ▲. 
Color the rest of the book bag red.
Write Arthur's name on the nametag.
If you were choosing a new book bag, what color would it be? _____

Reading for Information/Deductive Reasoning

Arthur ran out the front door with his book bag.
"Have a great day at school," said Mother.
"Stay as long as you want," said D.W.
Arthur's friends were also getting ready for school.

Write each person's name on the line below each house.

_____   _____   _____   _____

Arthur's house has a blue roof and a white fence.

Francine's house has red flowers in front of it.

Buster does not live beside Francine.

Draw a brown dog in front of the Brain's house.

4

TM and © 1999 Marc Brown. All Rights Reserved.

Sequencing

Francine was first to the bus stop. Then, came Buster. Soon, everyone was there.

"I want the front seat," said Francine. "It's the best seat on the bus."

"I want the back seat," said Buster. "It's the bounciest."

The door of the bus opened. All the children walked to their seats.

Follow Arthur's bus. Draw a line in the maze. Follow the directions to see where the bus goes.

1. First, it went to the park.
2. Then, it went to the store.
3. Next, it went to the bank.
4. Last, it went past the ballfield.

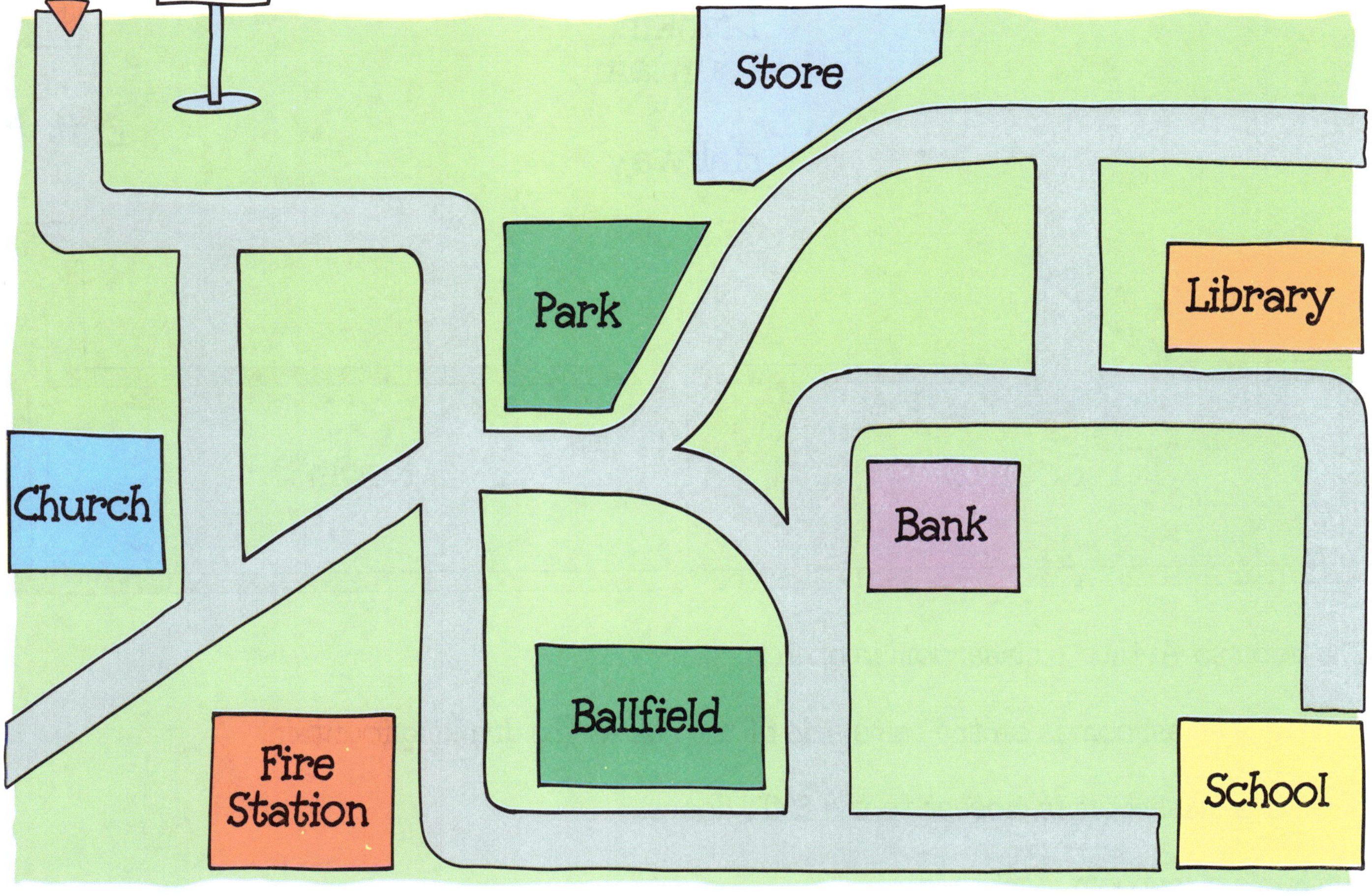

TM and © 1999 Marc Brown. All Rights Reserved.

Reading for Information/Deductive Reasoning

The school was busy. The halls were full of kids.
"Where is Mr. Ratburn's room?" Arthur asked.
Buster and Francine looked with Arthur.
"Maybe we should go back home," said Buster.

Use the clues to find Arthur's classroom.

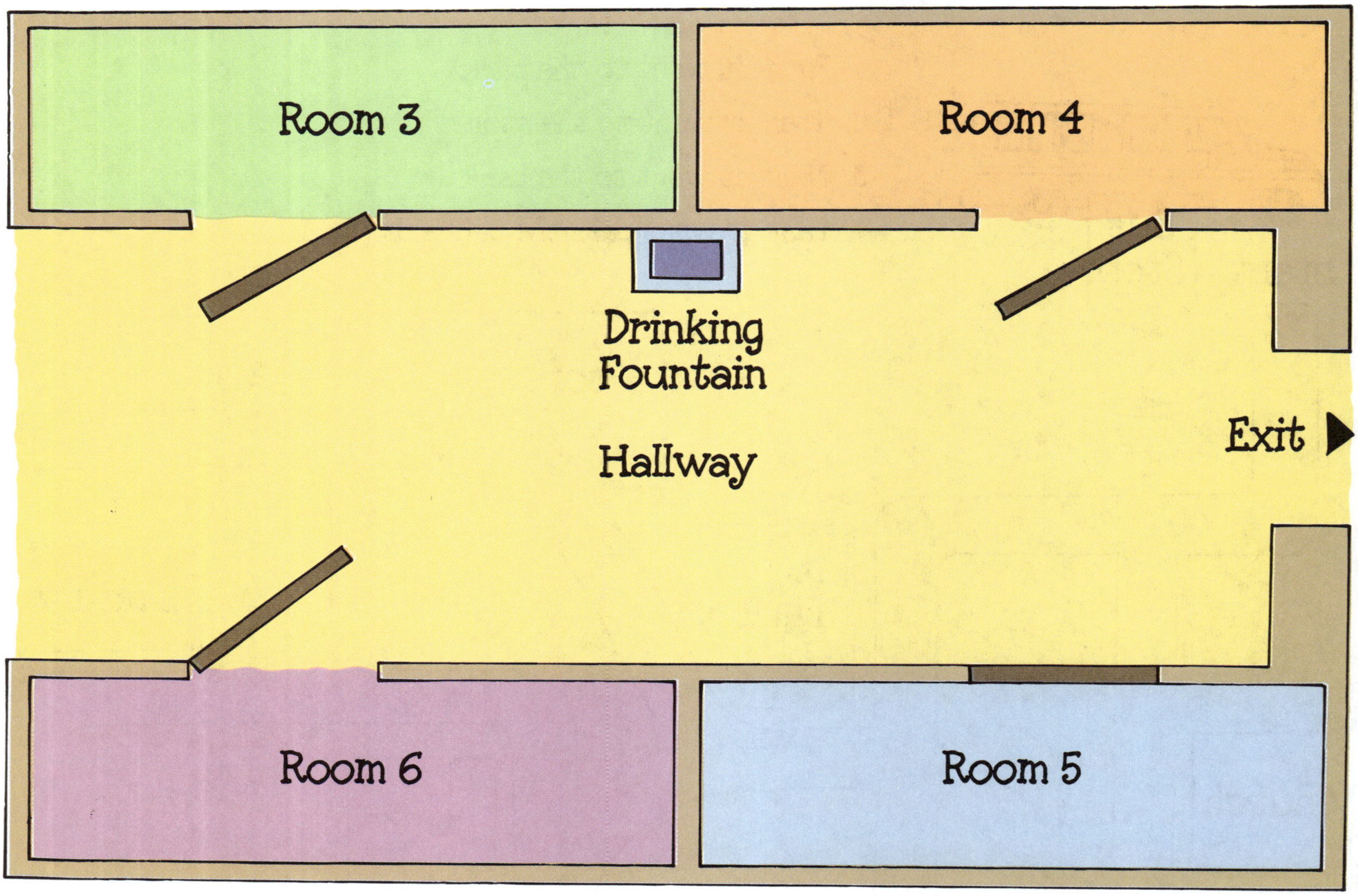

[Map showing Room 3 and Room 4 on the top side of the hallway (with Drinking Fountain), and Room 6 and Room 5 on the bottom side. Exit is on the right.]

The door to Arthur's classroom is open.

Arthur's classroom is on the same side of the hall as the drinking fountain.

Arthur's classroom is closest to the EXIT doors.

Arthur's classroom number is _____.

Word Recognition: Beginning Sounds

"Welcome to Room 4," said Mr. Ratburn, standing at the door. "We have a special classroom with lots to do. Just look around. See all the fun things we will be working with this year."

Label the things in Arthur's classroom. Write the correct word under each picture.

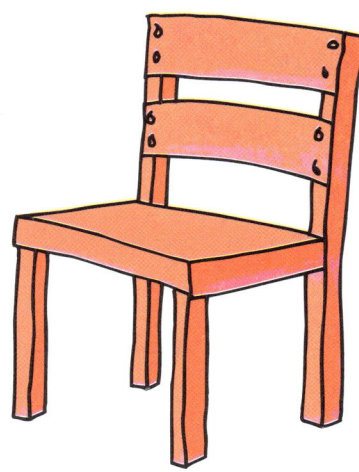

easel   chair   rug   window   books   table

Sight Words/Reading Words in Context

Mr. Ratburn called the class to the rug.

"This year, we will read many things together. Today, I wrote you a special letter, but I left out some words. Let's read it and see what is missing."

Read Mr. Ratburn's letter. Help Arthur's class write the missing words. Use the words in the box to help you.

Dear Class,

Welcome _____ first grade!

Today _____ the first _____ of school. We _____ learn a lot _____ year. _____ will also _____ a lot of fun!

Have a _____ day today!

Love,
Mr. Ratburn

this	is
we	have
to	good
day	will

Word Identification

Then, Mr. Ratburn said, "Let's learn a little more about each other. When I call your name, please tell the class something about you. Arthur?"

"A lot of my friends are in my class this year," said Arthur.

"Well, that's nice," said Mr. Ratburn. "Why don't you name them."

Help Arthur name all of his Room 4 friends. Find their names in the word search below. Find Arthur's name, too.

ARTHUR   FRANCINE   BINKY

BUSTER   MUFFY   BRAIN

O	C	B	X	W	O	R	P
K	C	A	R	T	H	U	R
M	Z	Q	P	A	O	C	D
U	B	U	S	T	E	R	H
F	R	A	N	C	I	N	E
F	A	C	R	A	B	K	E
Y	I	X	B	I	N	K	Y
L	N	C	G	H	K	J	A

TM and © 1999 Marc Brown. All Rights Reserved.

Following Directions

"Today, each of you will make a picture that will tell the class more about you," said Mr. Ratburn. "Get your crayons ready."

"I hope it tells me who brought something good to eat for lunch," said Binky. "I'm *starving*! Isn't it time to eat yet?"

Follow the directions to make a house that tells about you.

1. Color the roof red if you are a girl.
   Color it blue if you are a boy.

2. Draw a yellow door if your hair is blond.
   Draw a black door if your hair is black.
   Draw a brown door if your hair is brown.
   Draw a red door if your hair is red.

3. Draw a tall chimney if you wear glasses.
   Draw a short chimney if you do not wear glasses.

4. Draw a window for each person who lives in your house.

5. Draw a tree beside the house if you have a pet.
   Draw red flowers beside the house if you do not have a pet.

6. Write your address at the bottom of the page.

7. Color the house with your favorite color.

8. Add some other things to make your house special!

Following Directions

Reading for Information/Deductive Reasoning

"That was interesting," said the Brain. "Look at my house."

"Here is what mine looks like," said Buster.

Then, Mr. Ratburn said, "Here is a list of school supplies. You will need to bring these to class tomorrow."

Mr. Ratburn handed out the list, but everything on it was a riddle.

Help Arthur and his classmates solve the school supply riddles.

1. This wood is thin.
   You hold it tight.
   Keep it sharp.
   It helps you write.
   It is a _____.

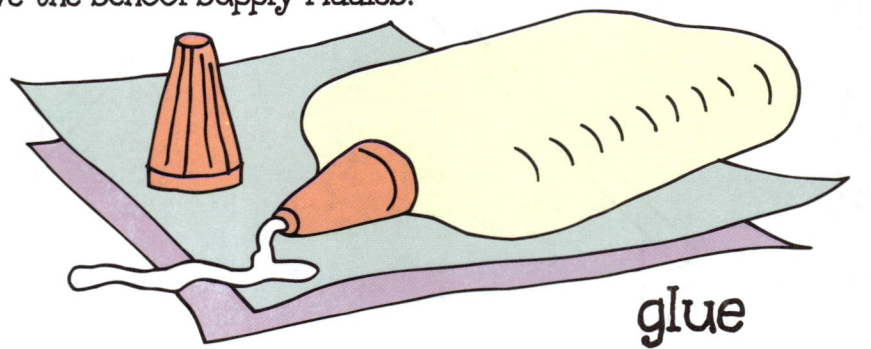
glue

ruler

2. It has a zipper.
   It has a pack.
   Books go inside.
   It sits on your back.
   It is a _____.

3. It comes in a bottle.
   It is sticky and white.
   It holds things together,
   And stays out of sight.
   It is _____.

crayons

12

TM and © 1999 Marc Brown. All Rights Reserved.

Reading for Information/Deductive Reasoning

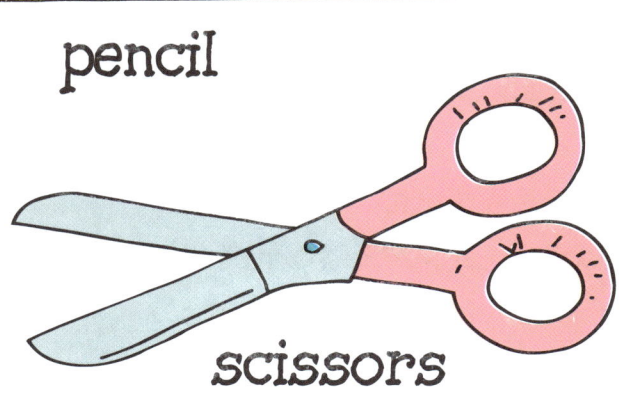
pencil

scissors

4. To make a good picture,
   You need some of these.
   Take one from the box.
   Then, color what you please!
   They are _____ .

paints

5. It is long.
   It is straight.
   For measuring,
   It works great.
   It is a _____ .

book bag

6. They come with a brush
   And sit in a row.
   Mix them with water
   To make colors flow.
   They are _____ .

Letter/Sound Correspondence

"Let's be sound detectives," said Mr. Ratburn.
Arthur thought being a detective would be fun.
"Look around the room," said Mr. Ratburn.
"I see a map, a door and a book. Over there is a plant."
"Here is a pencil," said Binky.
"Good," said Mr. Ratburn. "Let's write the ending sounds for some of these things."

Be a sound detective! Fill in the ending sounds for these words. Choose one of the letters at the bottom of the page.

fla____

ma____

doo____

penci____

plan____

boo____

k   l   p   r   g   t

Sight Words/Rhyming

The class started matching colors and color words. Arthur was still thinking like a sound detective. He tried to think of words that rhymed with the color words.

"Arthur, are you with us?" asked Mr. Ratburn.

"Oh, yes," said Arthur. And then he thought, "And I'm way ahead, too."

Help Arthur match each color word to a word that rhymes with it. Then, fill in the circle with the color it names.

○ red

○ black

○ green

○ white

○ pink

Compound Words

"Oh, boy! Recess!" yelled Arthur.
"It's about time," said Binky. "I need to run around."
Everyone headed for the playground. It was packed.
"What should we do first, Arthur?" asked Buster.
Arthur looked at all the things to do. He could not decide.
"We need to get logical," said the Brain. "Let's make a list."

baseball

football

basketball

slide

soccer

swingset

kickball

tag

TM and © 1999 Marc Brown. All Rights Reserved.

TM and © 1999 Marc Brown. All Rights Reserved.

Compound Words

When the Brain wrote his list, he saw that there were many compound words on it. He showed them to Arthur.

"What are compound words?" asked Arthur. "They sound hard."

"They're easy," said the Brain. "Two small words make one big word."

"Oh, cool," said Buster.

Fill in the Brain's list with compound words. First, write the compound word. Then, write the two small words that make up each compound word.

1. _____playground_____   4. _____

   ___play___ ___ground___   _____ _____

2. _____   5. _____

   _____ _____   _____ _____

3. _____   6. _____

   _____ _____   _____ _____

Can you think of other compound words? Try to find other compound words on your own. Write them below.

_____   _____

_____   _____

Letter/Sound Correspondence

The first thing after recess was music class.
"I love music," Arthur told Binky.
Binky whistled. Then, he said, "So do I."
"Everyone come up and choose an instrument,"
said Miss Krasny, the music teacher.

Write the correct blend to finish the name for each instrument. Then, write an **A** by the instrument you think Arthur chose. Write a **B** by the instrument Binky chose.

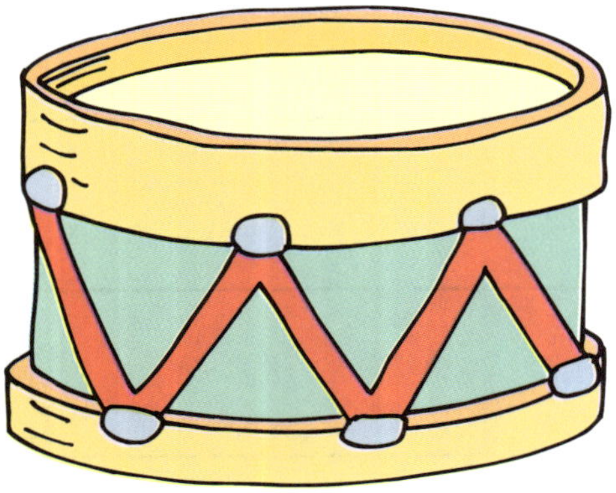

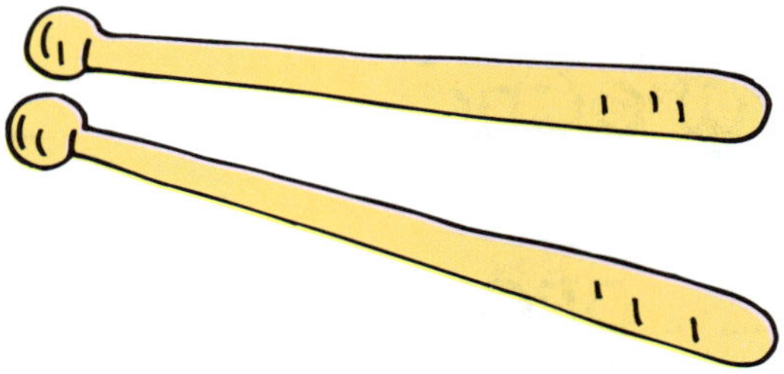

_____ icks

_____ um

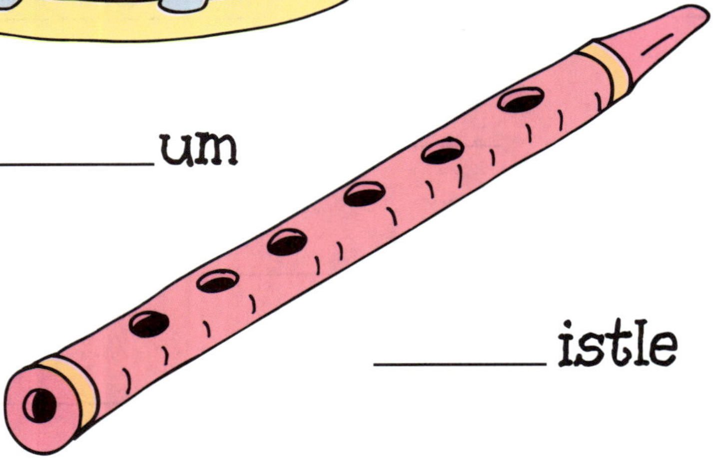

_____ istle

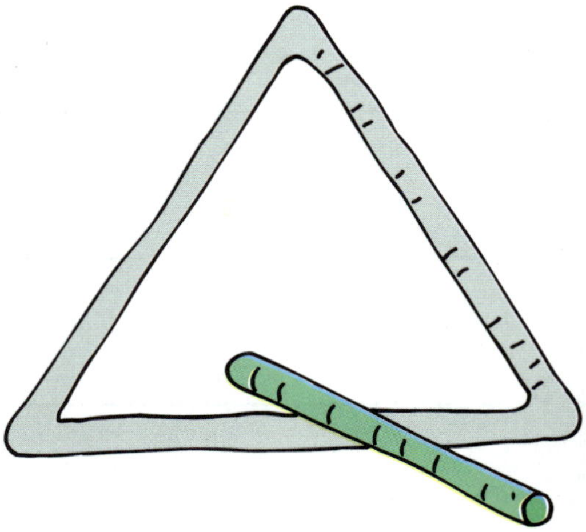

_____ iangle

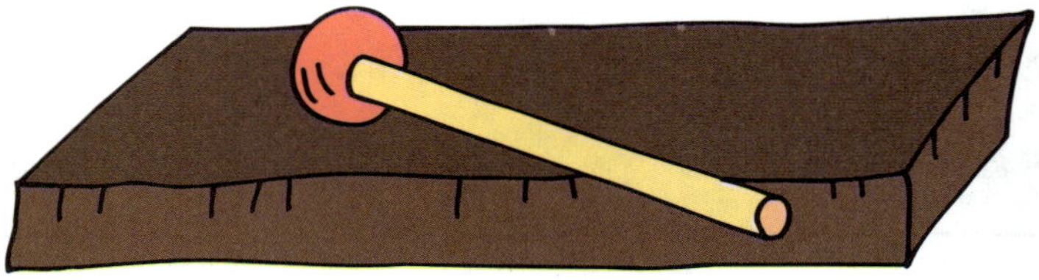

wood _____ ock

18   TM and © 1999 Marc Brown. All Rights Reserved.

Matching Characters/Titles

In the school library, Arthur's class found many books they liked.

"I found twelve books on baseball," said Binky.

"Here is a book about horses," said Muffy.

Arthur picked four books from the shelves.

"What can you tell me about these books?" asked Miss Turner, the librarian.

Help Arthur by matching the characters with the books. Draw a line between them.

The Three Bears

The Three Little Pigs

The Gingerbread Boy

Little Red Riding Hood

Which of these books have you read? Circle the book you like best.

19

TM and © 1999 Marc Brown. All Rights Reserved.

ABC Order

"Lunchtime," announced Mr. Ratburn.

"Oh, boy!" cheered Buster.

"Finally," said Muffy.

"I'm hungry," said Binky. "I'm playing football and I have to keep up my strength."

Arthur stood in line. He read the lunch menu. The line was very long. Arthur tried to put the food names in ABC order.

Help Arthur put the food names in ABC order.

1. _____   4. _____

2. _____   5. _____

3. _____   6. _____

milk   carrots   orange

pizza   applesauce   beans

Categorizing

Now, write your own menu for a lunch you would like to eat.

1. fruit _____

2. vegetable _____

3. meat _____

4. milk _____

5. bread _____

6. sweets _____

TM and © 1999 Marc Brown. All Rights Reserved.

Sight Words/Numbers

Coach Krensky started gym class with exercises.

"You must be kidding! This is the first day of school!" complained Muffy. "There is just so much we can do in one day."

"Let's get to it! No slackers!" barked the coach.

Coach Krensky showed the class how many of each exercise to do. As the kids finished each one, they checked it off on a list.

Write the correct number words on Coach Krensky's clipboard. Try the exercises yourself. Check each box when you are done.

10	5	7
_____ ☐	_____ ☐	_____ ☐
jumping jacks	push-ups	toe touches
8	6	3
_____ ☐	_____ ☐	_____ ☐
sit-ups	squats	laps around the gym

two   seven   nine   five   one
three   four   eight   ten   six

Opposites

Back in class, Arthur and Francine worked in the science corner.

"Let's see how good you are at observing," said Mr. Ratburn.

"I observe best with my movie star glasses," said Francine.

Help Arthur and Francine finish their observations. Write the correct opposite word on each line.

big _____

tall  _____   in _____

hard  _____   light _____

Can you think of any other opposites? Write down five more on another piece of paper.

Classification Skills

"I can't wait for art class," Binky said.

"I hope we don't do sit-ups in art," said Muffy.

"Be sure to put on a paint shirt to protect your clothes," said Miss Bryan, the art teacher. "Today we are going to mix paint and create new colors."

Color the Venn diagrams below. Write the new colors Arthur and his friends made.

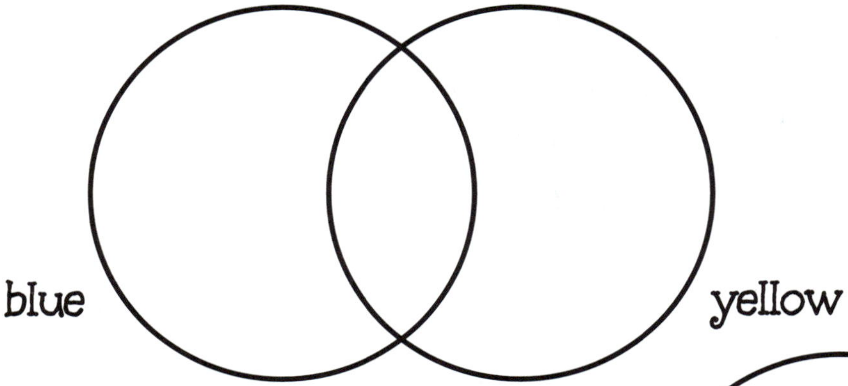

blue   yellow

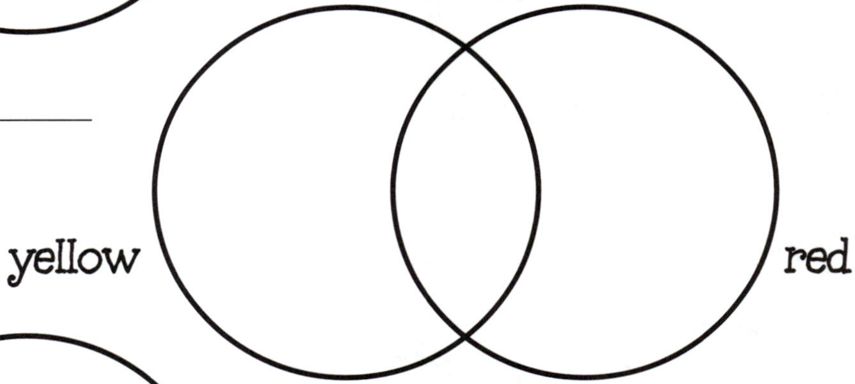

_____

yellow   red

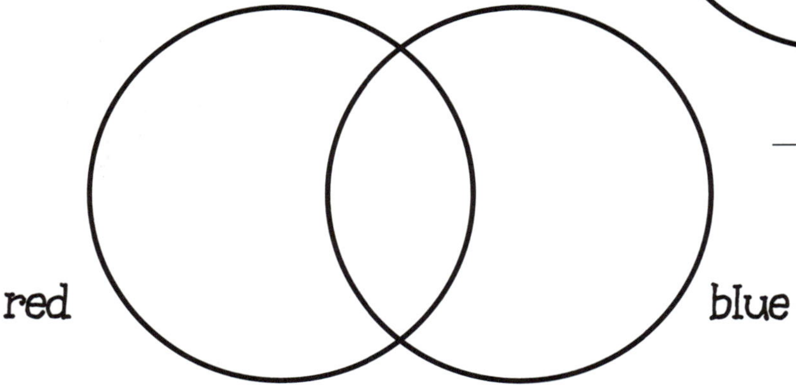

_____

red   blue

_____

Classification Skills

Mr. Ratburn also used Venn diagrams back in Room 4. But he used them to compare other things.

"Today, we will compare apples and bananas," he said.

"This will be easy," thought Arthur. "It's just like mixing colors, only now we're using words."

What are some words that describe apples? Write them here.

What are some words that describe bananas? Write them here.

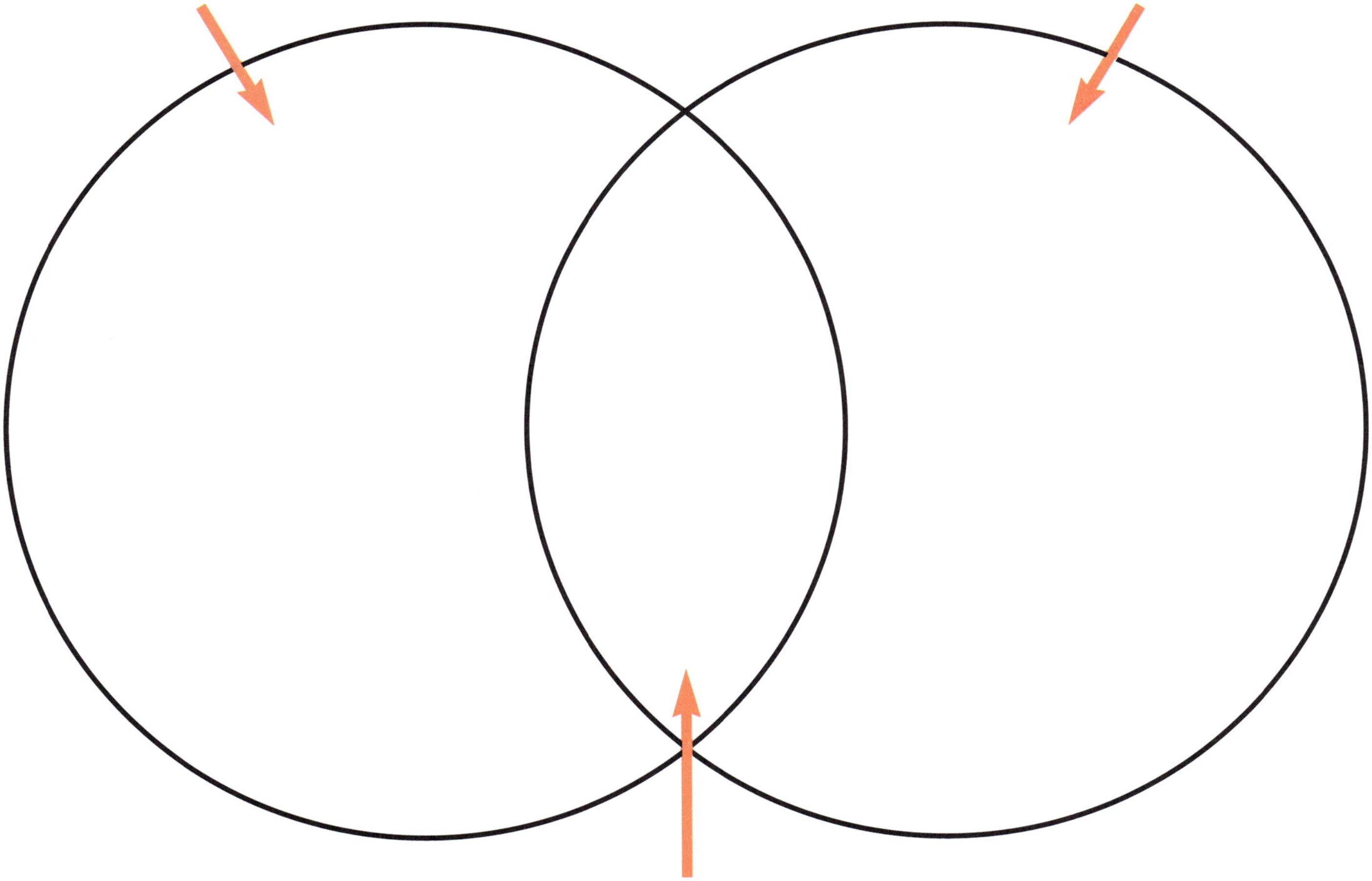

What are some words that describe both apples and bananas? Write them here.

Deductive Reasoning

"Every month we will have a pet day," Mr. Ratburn told the class.
"There had better not be any snakes," said Francine.
The Brain winked at Binky. Binky winked at Arthur. Arthur hissed.

Read the clues to find out which pets are coming to school. Circle the correct pictures.

It cannot fly.
It has whiskers.
It has long ears.

It has on a red collar.
It is not a puppy.

It is green.
It has four legs.
It has a shell.

Will Francine have to worry about snakes at school? _____

Contractions

Suddenly, the bell rang.

"Gather your things," said Mr. Ratburn. "It's time to go."

Arthur and all of the kids in Room 4 hurried to get ready. Then, the bell rang again.

"Hooray!" they yelled.

Write the correct contractions in these speech bubbles. Use the Word Box.

_____ time to leave.
It is

_____ going home!
We are

_____ forget your backpack.
Do not

_____ go!
Let us

_____ your hat.
Here is

| Don't | It's | Isn't |
| Here's | Let's | We're |

27

Conclusion

"You made it back alive," said D.W. when Arthur got home.

"Well, what did you think of school?" Mother asked.

"It was fun!" Arthur said.

"What kinds of things did you do?" asked Father.

"I got to be a sound detective," said Arthur. "And Mr. Ratburn said I could bring Pal in on Pet Day. We learned a lot."

"So, do you like first grade?" asked Mother.

"No," said Arthur, "I *love* it!"

Glossary of Skills

Arthur at School includes the following first grade reading skills:

ABC Order: The process of sequencing letters and words in the order of the alphabet. Alphabetizing is a basic organizational skill.

Categorizing: The process of sorting similar words and concepts into groups. Categorizing is an important organizational and thinking skill and aids in problem solving.

Classification Skills (Venn Diagram): A diagram used to identify attributes and to help compare and contrast. A Venn diagram involves observation and thinking skills that are important to problem solving.

Compound Words: A single word made up of two other distinct words. Looking for smaller words in larger words helps in decoding.

Contractions: The shortening of two words into one word with the same meaning. Contractions are commonly used in reading, writing and speech.

Following Directions: Performing prescribed activities to demonstrate reading understanding. The ability to follow directions is an important reading comprehension and life skill.

Letter/Sound Correspondence: Recognizing that letters and letter combinations represent different sounds, and placing those sounds in the correct sequence in a word. Using letter/sound correspondence is necessary for decoding words when reading.

Matching Characters/Titles: The identification of characters in books. Recognition of specific characters from stories is developed by familiarity with a wide range of reading materials.

Opposites: Words that are exactly the reverse in meaning from other words. Identifying opposites is an important thinking and comprehension skill.

Reading for Information/Deductive Reasoning: Information from reading used to help reason and form logical conclusions. Deductive reasoning is a critical thinking skill necessary for problem solving.

Glossary of Skills

Rhyming: Words that have the same ending sound. Rhyming helps beginning readers see relationships between words, which aids in decoding new words.

Sequencing: Recognizing an order of events and understanding how to put events in order. Sequencing is important in reading comprehension and aids in predicting what may happen in a story.

Word Identification: The ability to recognize letter patterns that form words. Recognizing letter patterns requires readers to develop an attention to detail and proper spelling.

Words in Context: The use of words and sentence structure to help figure out unknown words while reading. Context is an additional strategy used for decoding unknown words as well as an aid in comprehension.

Word Recognition/Sight Words: Words that are recognized immediately upon seeing them. The ability to recognize words on sight is necessary for reading fluency and comprehension.

Page 2.

Page 3.

Sample:

Page 4.

Page 5.

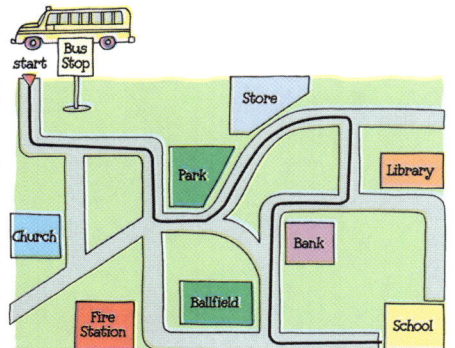

Page 6.

Arthur's classroom number is 4 .

Page 7.

Page 8.

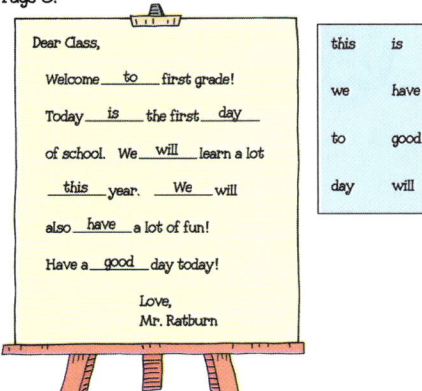

Dear Class,
Welcome __to__ first grade!
Today __is__ the first __day__
of school. We __will__ learn a lot
__this__ year. We will
also __have__ a lot of fun!
Have a __good__ day today!
       Love,
       Mr. Ratburn

this	is
we	have
to	good
day	will

Page 9.

	ARTHUR		FRANCINE		BINKY	
BUSTER		MUFFY		BRAIN		
O	C	B	X	W	O	R	P
K	C	A	R	T	H	U	R
M	Z	Q	P	A	O	C	D
U	B	U	S	T	E	R	H
F	R	A	N	C	I	N	E
F	A	C	R	A	B	K	E
Y	I	X	B	I	N	K	Y
L	N	C	G	H	K	J	A

Page 11.

Answers will vary.

Page 12.

1. pencil
2. bookbag
3. glue

Page 13.

4. crayons
5. ruler
6. paints

Page 14.

fla __g__   doo __r__   ma __p__
plan __t__ boo __k__   penci __l__

Page 15.

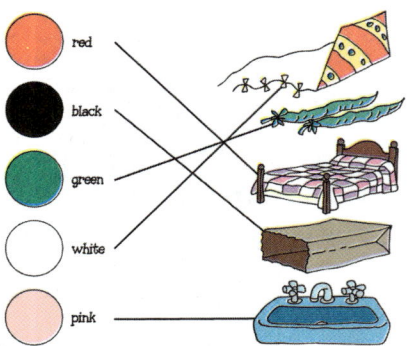

Page 17.

1. playground; play ground
2. baseball; base ball
3. football; foot ball
4. basketball; basket ball
5. swingset; swing set
6. kickball; kick ball.
   Other answers will vary.

Page 18.

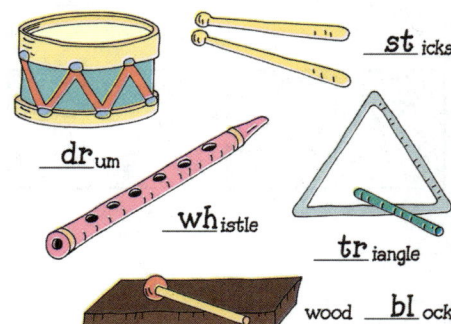

Page 19.

Page 20.

1. applesauce
2. beans
3. carrots
4. milk
5. orange
6. pizza

Page 21.

Answers will vary.

Page 22.

Page 23.

Page 24.

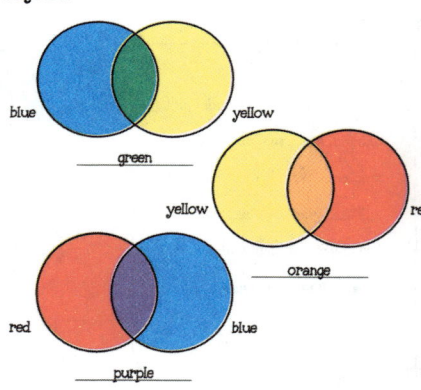

Page 25.

Answers may include:

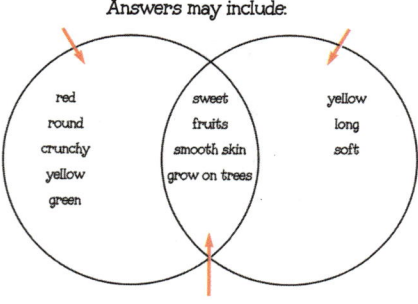

Page 26.

Page 27.

32

TM and © 1999 Marc Brown. All Rights Reserved.